Read-Along
STORYBOOK AND CD

This is the story of two sisters named Anna and Elsa. You can read along with me in your book. You will know it is time to turn the page when you hear this sound. . . . Let's begin now.

For more Disney Press fun, visit www.disneybooks.com

 PRESS

New York • Los Angeles

When Princess Elsa and Princess Anna of Arendelle were little girls, they were the best of friends. Anna was one of the only people who knew Elsa's secret: Elsa had the power to make snow and ice with just her hands!

One night, Elsa filled an empty ballroom with snow. The sisters played together, building a snowman, sledding, and ice skating.

But as they played, Elsa lost control. She accidentally hit Anna with a blast of icy magic! Anna was badly hurt, so her parents went to the ancient mountain trolls for help. There, a wise old troll told them that Anna could be saved—she was lucky to have been hit in the head, not the heart.

Even though Anna got better, her parents worried that people would fear Elsa's powers. To keep her gift a secret, they surrounded the castle with walls and never let anyone inside.

But whenever Elsa had strong feelings, the magic still spilled out. Elsa didn't want to hurt her sister again, so she never played with Anna. That made Anna feel very lonely.

Even after their parents were lost in a storm at sea, the sisters didn't spend any time together.

Years later, it was time for Elsa to become queen of Arendelle. For just that day, the castle gates were opened! Hundreds of people attended the crowning ceremony. Elsa worked hard to hide her feelings—and her powers!

Anna loved meeting all the new people. "I wish it could be like this all the time."

"Me, too."

At the coronation party, Anna danced with handsome
Prince Hans from the Southern Isles. He made her heart
flutter. It seemed like they had everything in common.

Because the gates were just open for one day, Hans and Anna knew this was their only chance to be together. "Can I say something crazy? Will you marry me?"

"Yes!"

Anna and Hans asked Elsa for her blessing. But Elsa thought their engagement was a bad idea. "You can't marry a man you just met. My answer is no."

Anna couldn't believe it. "Why do you shut me out? What are you so afraid of?"

Elsa started to lose control. "Enough!" As she
shouted, ice shot from her hands. Everyone stared
at Elsa in shock. Now all of Arendelle knew Elsa's
secret! Elsa panicked and fled for the mountains.

Anna felt horrible! Elsa's out-of-control powers had created
a terrible winter storm—in the middle of summer! "I'll bring her
back, and I'll make this right." She left Hans in charge of the
kingdom, and raced after Elsa on her horse.

But as Anna rode through the fierce wind, her horse threw
her into the snow and ran off back to Arendelle.

Luckily, Anna met an ice harvester named Kristoff
and his reindeer friend Sven. She asked them for help.
"I know how to stop this winter."
Together, they set off to look for Elsa.

As they climbed the mountain, Anna and Kristoff discovered a beautiful winter wonderland. There, they met an enchanted snowman named Olaf. Anna thought he looked familiar. "Olaf, did Elsa build you?"

Olaf smiled. "Yeah. Why?"

"Do you know where she is?"

"Yeah. Why?"

Kristoff got to the point. "We need Elsa to bring back summer."

Olaf was eager to help them. "Come on!"

Meanwhile, Hans was hard at work helping the people of Arendelle. But when Anna's horse came back to the castle without her, Hans knew he couldn't stay.

"Princess Anna is in trouble." Hans turned to the crowd. "I need volunteers to go with me to find her!" Soon, Hans and some soldiers set out in search of Anna—and Elsa.

Back on the mountain, Olaf led Anna and Kristoff to a giant ice palace that Elsa had created with her powers.

Even Kristoff was impressed. "Now that's ice."

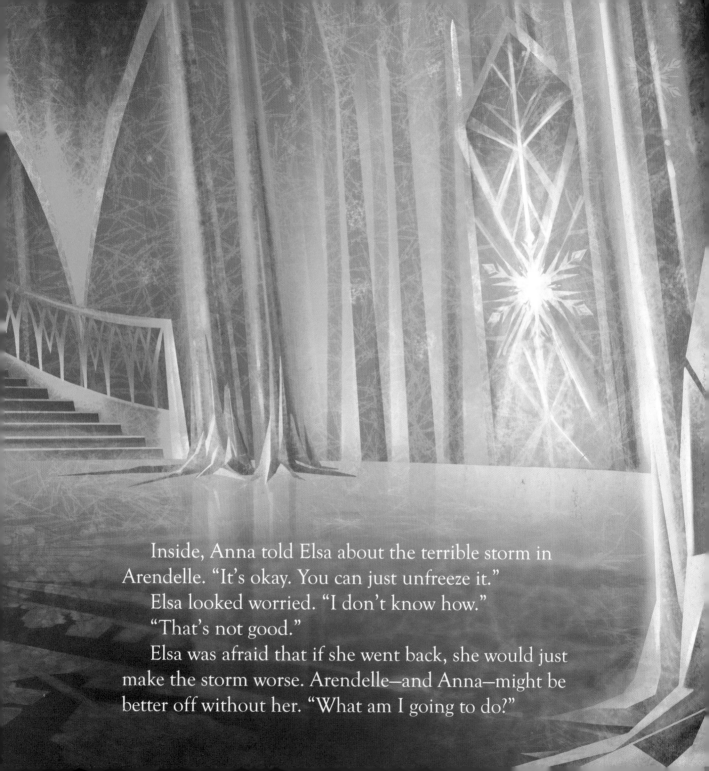

Inside, Anna told Elsa about the terrible storm in Arendelle. "It's okay. You can just unfreeze it."

Elsa looked worried. "I don't know how."

"That's not good."

Elsa was afraid that if she went back, she would just make the storm worse. Arendelle—and Anna—might be better off without her. "What am I going to do?"

Anna tried over and over again to convince Elsa to come home. But Elsa was too scared that she would hurt more people. As Elsa argued with her sister, an icy wave of magic burst from her body—and struck Anna in the chest! "Anna!"

Anna stood up and looked at Elsa. "No. I'm not leaving without you, Elsa."

"Yes, you are." Elsa knew what she had to do.

Elsa used her magic to create a huge snowman. He chased the friends out of the palace and toward a tall cliff.

Kristoff pulled out a rope to help them climb down.

"What if we fall?"

"There's twenty feet of fresh powder down there. It will be like landing on a pillow . . . hopefully."

They leaped over the edge, and landed safely on the fluffy snow below. They had escaped from the snowman, but Anna had other things to worry about. . . .

Anna's hair was turning snowy white!

"It's because she struck you, isn't it?" Kristoff brought Anna to the trolls, hoping they could help. One troll told them that Elsa's icy magic had struck Anna's heart. If the magic was not reversed, Anna would soon be frozen solid. Only an act of true love could thaw a frozen heart.

Anna knew she loved Hans—maybe a kiss from him would work! As the friends hurried toward Arendelle, Anna began to shiver. Kristoff was especially worried about her. He was starting to care for Anna.

At that moment, Hans and his soldiers had arrived at the ice palace and attacked Elsa. As she defended herself, Elsa trapped one of her attackers behind icy spikes.

Hans cried out to her. "Queen Elsa! Don't be the monster they fear you are."

Elsa paused, but in her moment of doubt, she was knocked out. The attackers brought her back to Arendelle and threw her in the dungeon.

When Anna arrived in Arendelle, she said good-bye to Kristoff and Olaf. Then, she raced to see Hans.

As soon as they were alone, Anna asked Hans to save her with a kiss. But Hans refused! Anna realized that he had only pretended to love her. He wanted to take over Arendelle by getting rid of Anna and Elsa! "All that's left now is to kill Elsa and bring back summer."

Hans left Anna alone and shivering. Luckily, Olaf found her and helped her warm up by the fire. But Anna was still getting weaker and weaker.

As Anna told him about Hans's evil plan, Olaf glanced out the window and saw Kristoff racing toward the castle. He realized that Kristoff loved Anna. "There's your act of true love right there!" It was Kristoff that Anna needed to kiss! With the last of her strength, Anna struggled outside.

Meanwhile, Elsa had escaped from the dungeon, but Hans was close behind her. "Elsa, you can't run from this." Hans told Elsa about her magic blast to Anna's heart. "I tried to save her, but it was too late."

Elsa collapsed in the snow and closed her eyes. Everything she had done to protect her sister had failed. And it was all her fault.

Nearby, Anna was hurrying toward Kristoff when she heard the clang of Hans's sword. She turned and saw her sister—Elsa was in danger!

Instead of saving herself and running to Kristoff, Anna leaped in front of her sister. "No!"

As Hans swung his sword, it shattered against Anna's frozen body. She had turned to solid ice.

Elsa clutched her sister. "Oh, Anna. No. Please, no!"
Suddenly, Anna began to thaw! Her arms, warm again, reached
around Elsa, and the two sisters hugged.

As Olaf watched them, he remembered what the wise old
troll had said: "An act of true love will thaw a frozen heart."
Anna's love for Elsa had saved both of them—and the kingdom.

Soon the two sisters were best friends again, and summer had returned to Arendelle. Elsa even made Olaf a little snow cloud to keep him from melting.

One day, Elsa had a surprise for Anna—the castle gates were wide open! "We are never closing them again."

The sisters smiled at each other. Now everything was the way it was supposed to be.